READ ALL THESE

NATE THE GREAT

DETECTIVE STORIES

BY MARJORIE WEINMAN SHARMAT

WITH ILLUSTRATIONS BY MARC SIMONT
(*unless otherwise noted*)

Nate The Great
and The
Big Sniff

by Marjorie Weinman Sharmat
and Mitchell Sharmat

illustrations by Martha Weston
in the style of Marc Simont

Delacorte Press

Published by
Delacorte Press
an imprint of
Random House Children's Books
a division of Random House, Inc.
1540 Broadway
New York, New York 10036

Visit us on the Web! www.randomhouse.com/kids
Educators and librarians, for a variety of teaching tools,
visit us at www.randomhouse.com/teachers

LIBRARY OF CONGRESS CATALOGING-IN-PUBLICATION DATA
Sharmat, Marjorie Weinman.
  Nate the Great and the big sniff / by Marjorie Weinman Sharmat and
Mitchell Sharmat ; illustrated by Martha Weston in the style of Marc Simont.
    p. cm.
  Summary: Nate the Great follows clues to find his lost dog, Sludge, in a
department store.
  ISBN 0-385-32604-1 (trade)   0-385-90020-1 (lib. bdg.)
  [1. Department stores—Fiction. 2. Dogs—Fiction. 3. Mystery and detective
stories.] I. Sharmat, Mitchell. II. Weston, Martha, ill. III. Title.
PZ7.S5299 Natd 2001
[E]—dc21   00-058971

The text of this book is set in 18-point Goudy Old Style.
Manufactured in the United States of America
September 2001
10 9 8 7 6 5 4 3 2
BVG

For our sweet, shaggy
DUDLEY SHARMAT
a.k.a.
DUDS
DIPSEY DOODLE
and
COMPUTER DOG
December 3, 1988 (adopted)–March 3, 1997
—M.W.S.
—M.S.

For Diane and Nancy, my good friends
—M.W.

Chapter One
The Long Wait

My name is Nate the Great.
I am a detective.
My dog, Sludge, is a detective too.
Today I had my biggest case ever.
But Sludge couldn't help me.
Because looking for Sludge
was the case!
Sludge was missing.
Lost. Gone.
I had to find him!
This morning Sludge and I
went out to shop.
We went to my favorite store,
Weinman Brothers.
Sludge isn't allowed in stores.

I go in and Sludge waits outside.
Sludge is great at waiting.
He likes to watch people go by.
He always finds a few
he likes to sniff.
"I am going to buy one thing,"
I said to Sludge.
"I will be right back."
Sludge wagged his tail
and sat down.

I walked into the store.

I was looking for a present for Sludge.

I went straight to the pet department.

I found a nice dog bowl.

And a long line of people.

They were all waiting to buy things.

I went to the end of the line.

9

Then I, Nate the Great, counted.
I was waiter number twenty-one.
I could grow old waiting in this line.
The seasons could change.
The world could change.
Pancakes could disappear.
And Sludge would still be waiting.
I put down the bowl.
I walked away. I went outside.

Sludge was gone!

Chapter Two
Slippy Sloppy Dog

I looked for Sludge.
I saw big puddles.
The air smelled of rain.
"Sludge!" I called.
"Woof!"
I heard a dog's bark.
I turned around.

Annie and her dog, Fang,
were standing there.
Fang is big and scary.
Today his teeth were wet
and gleaming.

"Are you looking
for Sludge?" Annie asked.
"I saw him sitting out here.
It started to rain.

Sludge got wet and drippy
and sloppy.
He moved closer to the store."
"So where is he?" I asked.
Annie pointed.
"He sat down on the thing
that opens the store door," she said.
"The door opened.
Sludge looked surprised.
He walked into the store."
"He walked *in*?" I asked. "Then what?"

"Sludge shook himself off.
He sat down and waited.
For you, I guess.
A saleslady came over with a towel.
She started to wipe him off.

Then another saleslady
yelled at him,
'You're not a shopper.
You have no money.
Leave!'
She grabbed Sludge.
But he slipped away.
'You slippy sloppy dog!'
she yelled after him."
"Then what happened?" I asked.

"Sludge ran into
the hat department.
I couldn't see him anymore.
So Fang and I went after him.
But the mean lady stopped us.
She looked at Fang and said,
'Too many teeth. Bad breath.
And no money. *Out!*'"
"Then what?"
"Fang growled at her.
She screamed and stepped back.

I took Fang outside.
A minute later you came along.
You missed Sludge."
"I must go to the hat department," I said.
"Fang and I will wait here," Annie said.
"In case Sludge comes back outside."
"He'd have to pass that lady,"
I said. "Sometimes Sludge is brave.
But not that brave."
"Well, Fang is.
He can go back in and get Sludge
past that lady.
He and I will guard the door.
If we get Sludge, we will find you."

Chapter Three
Hats and Underwear

I, Nate the Great,
rushed back into the store.
Annie called after me,
"Don't forget:
Sludge looks slippy sloppy.
It could be a clue."

I went to the hat department.
There were hats
of every size and shape.
But I did not see Sludge.
I looked for wet pawprints.
Perhaps there was a trail.
Nothing.
I went up to a salesman.
"There was a wet dog . . . ," I began.

The man pointed to the left.

"That way," he said.

I rushed to the underwear department.

No Sludge.

Could he be hiding from that mean lady?

But where could he hide?

I saw a sign: DRESSING ROOMS.

I did not want to peek into those rooms.

I did not want to look at underwear
with anyone inside it.

But I had to find Sludge.

I went to the dressing rooms.

"Sludge!" I called.

Somebody peeked out
from a dressing room.

Somebody who looked strange.

Very strange.

It was Rosamond.
She was wearing a nightshirt
that had MEOW
printed across the front.
It was much too small for her.
"I'm shopping," she said.
"This is for my cat Big Hex.
I buy all my cats' clothes here."

"Have you seen Sludge?" I asked.
"Yes," she said. "I saw him run
in and out of this department.
I don't blame him.
There's not a thing here for dogs."
"Thank you for that information," I said.
I left.
Where could Sludge have gone?

Chapter Four
Lost!
My Best Friend!

I needed clues.
I needed pancakes.
I always eat pancakes
when I can't solve a case.
They help me think.
I knew there was a cafeteria
at the back of the store.
They serve great pancakes.
But I did not want to go there.

I was not hungry.

I was sad.

I was thinking about Sludge.

How I had first met him.

In a field.

How he had become my dog.

And my best friend.

And now he was lost.

I went to a pay phone.

I called home.

The answering machine came on.

I left a message for my mother.

Dear Mother,
I am on my biggest
case. Sludge is lost.
I will be back. I hope
Sludge will be too.
Love,
Nate the Great

I hung up.
Where should I look next?
In this big store, who would know
where Sludge might be?
Of course!
I, Nate the Great, rushed to
the lost and found department.

Chapter Five

On the Run

I saw somebody I knew.
It was not Sludge.
It was Claude.
Claude spends a big part
of his life in lost and found.
The lost part.
Claude is always losing things.
I went up to him.

"I have lost Sludge," I said.

"I saw him," Claude said.

"Where?"

"At your house on Sunday," Claude said.

"He wasn't lost then," I said.

"Oh, right," Claude said.

Claude pointed to a man
sitting at a desk.

"He knows what's lost
and what's found.
Talk to him."

I rushed over to the man.
I said, "I, Nate the Great,
have lost my dog, Sludge,
in this store."
"Oh, the dog," the man said.
"We know about him.

He's been spotted
all over the place.
Nobody who sees him
will ever forget him,
I'll tell you that.
But we can't catch him.
He just runs and runs.
I haven't had a report
for five minutes.
He could be anywhere."
"Runs and runs?" I said. "Hmm."
"Hmm, what?" the man asked.
"A clue," I said.
I walked away.

Chapter Six
The Tip of a Tail

Sludge could be tired
by now, I thought.
Nobody has seen him
run for five minutes.
I rushed to the bed department.
It was full of beds.
A great place to rest!

I looked on the beds
and under them.
I looked for dog hairs
and pawprints.
And a dog.
Suddenly I saw what looked like
the tip of a tail!

It was under a bed.
Was I dreaming?
Was I hoping too hard?
I got closer.
It *was* a dog's tail!

And it was attached to Fang.
Fang crawled out
from under the bed.
Annie came running.
"There you are, Fang!" she yelled.
"What's Fang doing
in the store?" I asked.

"I thought I saw Sludge,"
Annie said. "So I ran inside.
Fang followed me."
"You saw Sludge?" I asked.
"No. It was a mistake.
It was a wet mop.
But don't worry.
I left the door guarded.
Rosamond came along.
She's standing there
with a big whistle."

"A whistle?"
"Yes. She said every guard
should have one."
I sat down on a bed.

"So Fang is the dog
who's been running
around the store," I said.
"And scaring the customers,"
Annie said.

I, Nate the Great, was sunk.
I should have guessed
that the running dog was Fang!
The man said that nobody
who saw him would ever forget him.
I should have known that was a clue.
The kind of clue I did not want to hear.

Chapter Seven
Think Like a Dog

Annie and Fang left.
I, Nate the Great,
lay down on the bed.
I was tired.
I had used my feet too much.
And my head too little.
I had to think.
Where would a *dog* go
in this store?
Suddenly I had the answer.

Kibbles, leashes, bowls,
doghouses, bones.
Where the good stuff was.
I rushed back to
the pet department.
I counted eleven people
still in line.
But Sludge wasn't one of them.
I went to the dog food.
No Sludge.
I went to the dog toys.
No Sludge.

I went to the doghouses.

Maybe Sludge would be asleep inside.

I looked in every one of them.

No Sludge.

Maybe Sludge had been here and left.

I walked up to the head of the line.

"Excuse me," I said

to the man behind the counter.

"I am in a hurry.

I am on a big case.

I am looking for a wet dog.

A slippy sloppy dog."

"A slippy sloppy dog?" he said.

"And it has a tail, right?"

I nodded.

"Fur?"

"Of course."

"And it barks?"

"Yes."

The man chuckled.

"Nice try," he said.

"But if you want to buy something
you have to go to the end of the line.

I remember you when you were
number twenty-one."
I, Nate the Great, walked away.
I sat down on a dog mat.
This was my most important case.
And I could not solve it.
Sludge always helped me
with my cases.

But now *he* was the case.
He could not help me.
Or could he?
Sludge was a great detective.

Was he trying to find *me*?
Was he sniffing
all over the store?
No. He was afraid the mean lady
would get him.
He had to hide.
But he had to find me too.
How could he do both things?
Suddenly I, Nate the Great,
had the answer.
Suddenly I knew where
Sludge had to be.

Chapter Eight
A Flour Trail

I rushed to the back of the store.
To the cafeteria.
Where the pancakes are.
People were sitting and eating.
There was a room
behind the cafeteria.
There was a trail of flour
going in and out of the room.
It was a trail of white pawprints.

The door of the room
was partway open.
I looked around.
No one was watching me.
I crept into the room.

It was a storeroom.
There were boxes and cans
and jars and sacks.
Sitting on a torn sack
of flour . . . was Sludge!

He was sniffing.
He rushed toward me.
He gave me a big sniff.
Then he wagged his tail.
And licked me all over.

"Sludge, you are a
great detective," I said.
"You knew I had a case to solve.
You knew I always eat pancakes
to help solve a case.
So you sniffed out
this pancake place
and you sat and waited.
You knew you could sniff me from your
hiding place when I showed up.
And that's what you did."
Sludge looked proud.
This had been *his* biggest case too.
I looked at the trail
of flour pawprints.
Did Sludge leave it on purpose?
Or did it just happen to happen?
I would never know.

But I didn't care.
I only cared that
I had found Sludge.
Or he had found me.
Whatever.
I said, "We both deserve
a treat. Wait here."

I went back to the cafeteria.
"Five pancakes to go," I said.
"And a bone."
I, Nate the Great,
and Sludge
sat on the torn sack of flour
and ate the best meal
we had ever had.